COME over to MY HOUSE

By Theo. LeSieg / Illustrated by Richard Erdoes

BEGINNER BOOKS   A Division of Random House, Inc.

COME over to MY HOUSE

Some houses are bricks
and some houses are sticks.

Some houses are square
and some houses are round.

There are all kinds of houses
around to be found.

4

Some are on stilts
high up off of the ground.

Some houses are wide.
Some houses are thin.
Some are so thin
you can hardly get in.

But wherever you go,
you will hear someone say,
"Come over to my house.
Come over and play!"

Come over to my house.
The fishing is great!
They bite all the time
and you don't have to wait.
Come over some day
and bring plenty of bait.

My house has a kite
that can whistle and sing!
Come over some day
and bring plenty of string.

My house has so many
big pine trees outside,
we can slide on my
wonderful pine needle slide.

The roof of my house

has a stork on a nest.

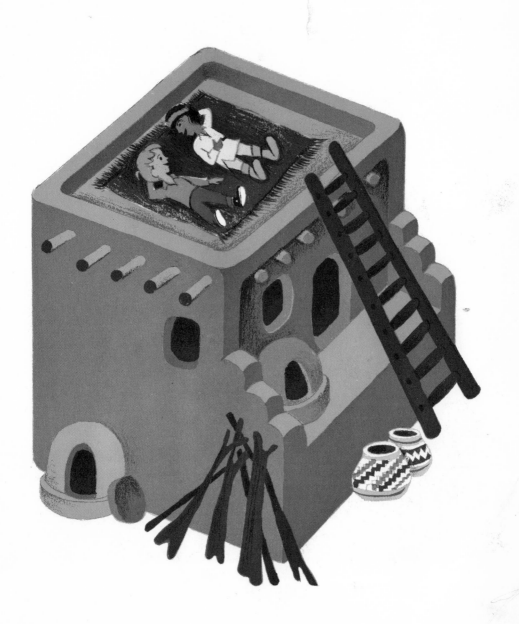

The roof of my house
is a good place to rest.

You can play on my roof.
But my house is so tall,
it's a long way downstairs
to go after the ball.

My house is bright pink
and it's happy and gay.
Our streets are wet water.
We like it that way.

Come up on my porch
and I'll give you a treat.
Spaghetti!
We'll eat
and we'll eat and we'll eat.
We'll eat twenty miles of it!
We'll eat a ton!
Food, at my house,
is such wonderful fun.

Come over to my house
and sit by the fire.

My fire burns trees
and it's hotter and higher.

Our fire's in a stove.

It makes beautiful heat.

Come over! Come over

and warm your cold feet.

Come over to my house.

I live on a boat.

I live in a city

of houses that float.

Come into my houseboat.
Have supper with me.
I'll give you cold rice
and a cup of hot tea.

I eat with chopsticks
and you can learn how.
But, boy, you are
terribly sloppy right now.

Come over to my house
and stay for the night.
We have 200 rooms
so I'm sure it's all right.

But don't touch the tigers.
They're liable to bite.

In my house, my bath
is a fancy machine
with handles and spouts
and it's long and it's green.

I just have a tub
but I keep just as clean.

At our house, hot water
comes out of the rocks.
It's handy for washing
ourselves and our socks.

34

Come over to our house.

You'll like our bath, too.

Especially if you have

some laundry to do.

Over at my house
you'll eat funny fruit.
You'll ride on my llama
and toot on my flute.

My house has books!
And they're all very fine.
I'll learn to read yours
if you'll learn to read mine.

עֲלֵיכֶם שָׁלוֹם בְּמִלּוֹת הֲסָדִים

39

In a faraway place,
in a wide empty land,
my house is a tent
in the wind and the sand.

At my house I'll show you
a wonderful show
in the night in the sky
when the Northern Lights glow.

My house has an ostrich.

Hop on! Take a ride.

But watch where you're riding!

Don't ride him inside!

In back of my house
lives a red kangaroo,
two koala bears,
also an emu or two.
Come over and play.
We're all waiting for you!

47

My house is quite cold.

I need fur to sleep in.

My house is quite hot.

I just sleep in my skin.

I sleep in a bed
with a big puffy puff.
Come over some night,
We have puff puffs enough.

50

In my house I sleep
on a mat on the floor.
There's a mat here for you.
But I hope you don't snore.

Come over to my house
and we'll milk a cow.
It isn't too hard
and it's time you learned how.

You can milk goats at my house
so come with your pail.
It's easy.
You'll find the milk
back near the tail.

My house has a reindeer.

Come on! Don't be shy.

Step up and start milking, boy.

Give it a try.

Every house in the world
has a ceiling and floor.
But the ones you'll like best
have a wide-open door.

Some houses are rich,
full of silver and gold.

And some are quite poor,
sort of empty and old.

Some houses are marble
and some are just tin.

But they're all,
all alike
when a friend
asks you in.

There are so many houses
you'll meet on your way.
And wherever you go,
you will hear someone say . . .

"Come over to my house!
Come over and play!"